Where is my bear?

Darcy Coxall

Menno Wittebrood

I climbed the wooden staircase
And clambered into bed,
But when I looked around for him
I couldn't find my Ted!

My bear was there this morning,
I'd left him safe and sound.
Someone must have taken him;
Now where could he be found?

First I peeked beneath my bed
And saw to my surprise,
Staring from the shadows
Was a pair of monster eyes!

"Have you seen Ted?" I softly said.
The creature answered, "No,
I have one here I'm cuddling,
But this bear is my own."

Out he came, all hair and horns,
With slippers on his feet.

He said, "Your bear cannot be far,
I'll help you find the thief!"

Off we went to look around,
Creeping through the night.
We headed for the chest of drawers,
Then ooooh! We got a fright!

From in between my pants and socks,
Something grabbed my wrist ...

... an alien came slinking out.
"What's going on?" it hissed.

"I've lost my Ted," I stuttered.
 It quickly set me free.
"A missing bear is not much fun,
 Let's see where he could be."

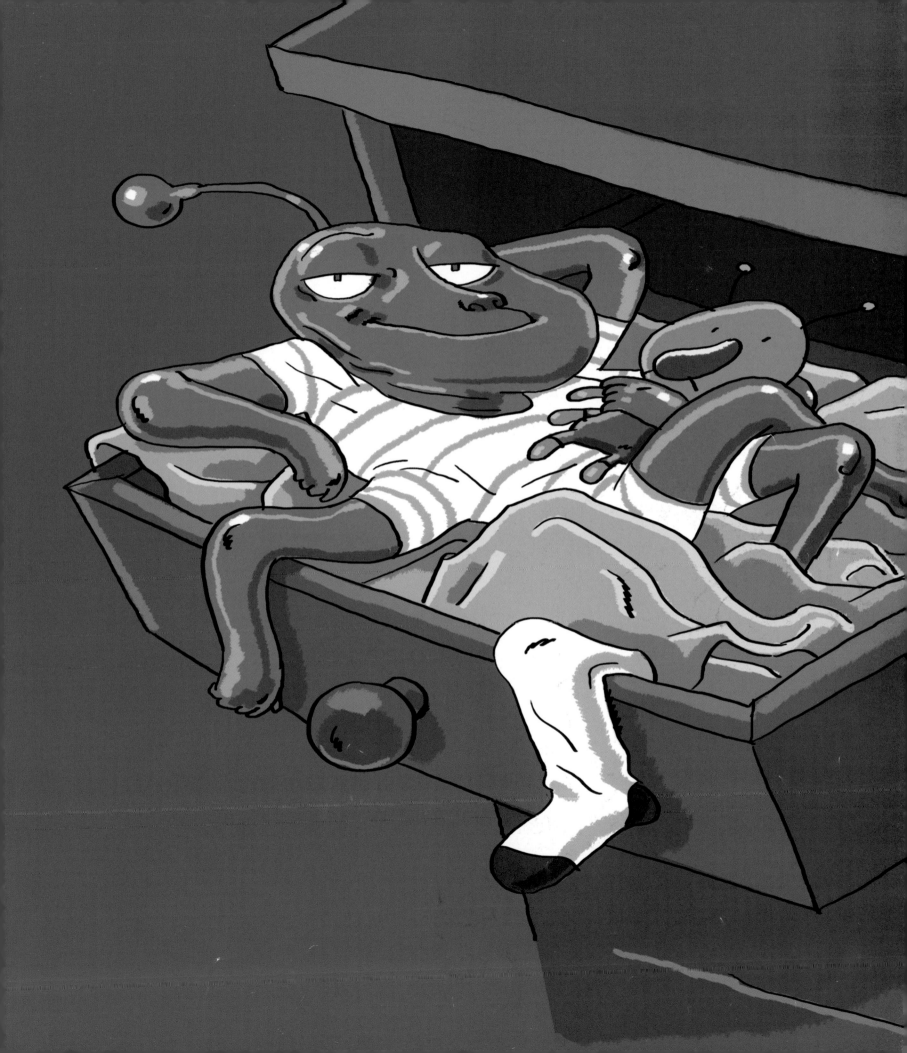

Off I went to search again
With monsters and their bears.
We headed for the wardrobe,
And an even bigger scare!

I pulled the doors wide open;
The hinges squeaked and squealed.

Behind a puff of light blue smoke
A dragon was revealed.

He huffed and puffed and shrugged and sighed:
"It's really rather shocking
To wake a dragon up like that,
You didn't think of knocking?"

"My Ted has gone," I told him.
He said, "That just won't do.
No one can sleep without a bear."
So he came looking too.

We searched behind the curtains
And every inch of floor.

We checked inside the toy box
And the bookcase by the door.

"Your Ted's not here," my new friends said,
"But wait, what's over there?
Does your bear have freckles
And messy long blond hair?"

I put my finger to my lips.
"That's not a bear," I said.
"It's Polly. Please don't wake her up!
Just tiptoe on ahead."

So the monsters and their teddies
Led me back to bed.
They tucked me in and patted me,
And told me not to fret.

"Borrow our three bears," they said,
"To help you sleep tonight.
We're sure you'll find your own again
Tomorrow, when it's light."

When I woke up, I rubbed my eyes
And checked just to be sure,
Next to me lay three strange bears
And stranger still – one more!

I grabbed my Ted and cuddled him,
His fur was fresh and clean.
I sniffed – he smelled all soapy,
Just guess where he had been?

For my girls - DC
For Maaike and Max - M.

Published by
Hogs Back Books
The Stables
Down Place
Hogs Back
Guildford GU3 1DE
www.hogsbackbooks.com
Printed in Singapore
ISBN: 978-1-907432-09-5
British Library Cataloguing-in-Publication Data.
A catalogue record for this book is available from the British Library.
1 3 5 4 2